Clifford
THE DOG WHO CRIED "WOOF!"

Adapted by Bob Barkly
Illustrated by John Kurtz

SCHOLASTIC

From the television script
"The Dog Who Cried 'Woof'" by Anne-Marie Perrotta and Tean Schultz

"It's a beautiful day," Cleo said.
"Let's play tag in the woods."

"Uh . . . I don't think so," Clifford said.
"Don't you know about Stinky the Skunk Ghost?"

"They say he haunts the woods!" T-Bone said.

"He's twenty feet tall. And he smells as bad as twenty skunks!"

"That's just a story," Cleo said.
"Don't you know Stinky isn't real?"

"Of course we do," Clifford said.

"Then what are we waiting for?" Cleo said.

"Clifford, you be It."

Cleo and T-Bone ran into the woods.
Clifford ran after them.
Cleo was fast . . .

but Clifford was faster.
He reached out to catch her.
"Look out behind you!" Cleo shouted.

Clifford stopped in his tracks.
So did T-Bone.
"What?" they asked.

"It's Stinky the Skunk Ghost!" Cleo cried.
Clifford and T-Bone spun around.
But no one was behind them.

Cleo fell over laughing.
"I fooled you!"

"That's not funny," said T-Bone.
"You scared us."

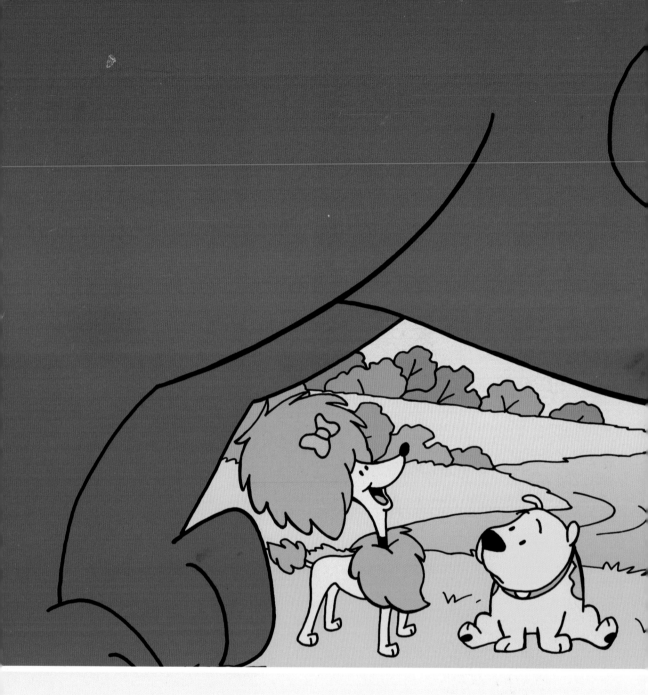

"I'm sorry," Cleo said. "But you guys *know* Stinky's not real. Let's go swimming."

SPLISH!

SPLASH!

They all jumped into the pond.

"Where's Cleo?" Clifford asked suddenly.
"She was here a minute ago," T-Bone said.

Just then, Cleo cried out from the woods.
"Help! Stinky the Skunk Ghost has got me!"

Clifford and T-Bone ran to the rescue.
They found Cleo all alone – alone and laughing.

"You fooled us again!" Clifford yelped.

"That wasn't nice."

"It was a joke," Cleo said.

Clifford and T-Bone were not amused.
They turned and walked away.

"Don't be angry," Cleo called after them.
"I'm sorry."

Cleo tried to catch up with her friends.
But her bow got caught on a branch.
"Help!" Cleo cried.

Clifford and T-Bone kept walking.
They thought Cleo was playing another trick.

Then they heard her cry out again.
Cleo sounded really scared.
And something smelt really bad.

"Ugh!" Clifford said. "That must be Stinky.
I bet he has Cleo."
Clifford and T-Bone ran back into the woods.

A skunk *did* have Cleo.

But this was no ghost.

This skunk was real – very real.

He left his stinky smell, then walked away.

T-Bone held his nose while Clifford set Cleo free.

"Thanks, guys," Cleo said. "I'm sorry I played those tricks on you."

Cleo ran home and had a bath.
Then she went to find her friends.

"I'll never trick you again," she promised.
"I've learned my lesson – the stinky way."

Other Clifford Storybooks:

The Big Egg Hunt
The Big Leaf Pile
The Mysterious Missing Dog Food
The Runaway Rabbit
The Show-and-Tell Surprise
Tummy Trouble

Clifford is also available on CD-ROM.
Clifford makes learning BIG fun with these new CD-ROMs for children aged 4 to 6:

Clifford Reading
Clifford Thinking Adventures
Clifford Learning Activities

Scholastic Children's Books
Commonwealth House, 1-19 New Oxford Street, London WC1A 1NU
a division of Scholastic Ltd
London ~ New York ~ Toronto ~ Sydney ~ Auckland ~ Mexico City ~ New Delhi ~ Hong Kong

First published in the USA by Scholastic Inc., 2001
First published in the UK exclusively for Marks and Spencer p.l.c. by Scholastic Ltd, 2002
This edition first published in the UK by Scholastic Ltd, 2002

ISBN 0 439 98248 0

3 4 5 6 7 8 9 10 Printed by Amadeus S.p.A. – Rome